GREY NECK

Inquiries should be directed to
Stemmer House Publishers, Inc.
2627 Caves Road
Owings Mills, Maryland 21117

Printed and bound in Singapore

A Barbara Holdridge book
First Edition

Library of Congress Cataloging-in-Publication Data

Rudolph, Marguerita.
  Grey neck.

  Adaptation of: Serafa Sheĭka / Mamin-Sibiriak, D.N.
  Summary: A young duck with a broken wing outwits a
hungry fox with the help of a kind hunter.
  [1. Folklore—Soviet Union] I. Kronz, Leslie
Shuman, ill. II. Mamin-Sibiriak, D.N. (Dmitriĭ
Narkisovich), 1852-1912.   Serafa Sheĭka.   III. Title.
PZ8.1.R85Gr 1988   398.2'452841'0947 [E]   88-2100
ISBN 0-88045-068-1

GREY NECK

by Marguerita Rudolph

Adapted from the Russian Tale of D.N. Mamin-Sibiryak

Illustrated by
Leslie Shuman Kronz

Stemmer
House

PUBLISHERS, INC.
OWINGS MILLS, MARYLAND

Nested among the reeds on a river bank in Northern Russia was a large family of ducks. Father and Mother Duck had chosen a safe home surrounded with thick shrubs. There they could care for their still helpless babies. They led the fluffy ducklings in a straight line to the river, where they could swim and feed all day long.

One of the ducklings was little Grey Neck — a lively one. Every now and then she liked to step out of line, to see what was there; then quickly get back in her place.

At night the mother kept all the ducklings under her warm wings. It was a cozy but crowded place and sometimes Grey Neck would slip out, but stay near by; then push her way back under Mother Duck. And all was well.

5

    Farther away, in the woods, lived Fox. He was a clever hunter, always on the lookout for some smaller creature that would make a meal for him. So he kept a close watch on the duck family. One night in the spring, just before dawn, Fox quietly made his way towards the ducks' home. Even in the dim light he spotted a duckling wandering by herself. It was Grey Neck. Losing no time, Fox crept silently, just close enough to grab hold of Grey Neck's soft wing.

Then, just as Fox turned to run off with the duckling, Mother Duck sensed danger to her baby. Instantly she threw herself fiercely at Fox, pecking him with her sharp beak and beating him on the head with her powerful wings, till Fox dropped the duckling and crawled away to lick his wounds.

Grey Neck's life was saved. But the wing that Fox had grabbed was broken. And although it healed soon enough, the wing no longer had flying power. Knowing that she would never be able to fly, Grey Neck felt very sad, especially when she saw other ducks going up into the air.

Still, she grew to be a healthy and lively young duck. All summer long there was no need for her to fly, and she stayed close to her family, enjoying life on the river. She could swim faster than any of her brothers and sisters. And when it came to diving — no one was better than Grey Neck. But the good summer came to an end.

With the first chill of autumn, the birds along the river edge began gathering in flocks for their yearly journey far to the south. The larger water birds — swans, geese and ducks — were taking their time; while the smaller shore birds — snipe, sand pipers and plovers — fluttered and flitted about, rushing from one shore to the other, flying over shallows and ponds with dazzling speed.

"Look at those small ones!" grumbled Father Duck. "What's their hurry? We'll all get ready to leave — soon enough."

"Not *all* of us," Mother Duck reminded him. "Not our little Grey Neck. You know she can't fly."

"Well, it can't be helped now," Father Duck answered.

"But I worry about leaving Grey Neck here alone. She might freeze," fretted Mother Duck. "Maybe I'll stay with her," she declared.

"And the other ducklings?"

"Nothing's wrong with them. They can manage without me."

"No! The others need you too, and so do I!" argued Father Duck.

Meanwhile Grey Neck watched the birds, and like them, she noticed the steady change in weather.

There had already been a number of cold mornings, and the hoar frost made the birches turn yellow and the aspens gold. The cold wind tore at the dry leaves and carried them away.

Every morning the young ducks went on flying excursions to strengthen their wings in readiness for the long journey. What noise! And what excitement!

Only Grey Neck could not take part in the comings and goings, and so she watched the other ducks from a distance.

"You'll come back in the spring — won't you?" Grey Neck asked her mother worriedly.

"Yes, yes, we'll all return…" Mother Duck was too upset to talk about it.

When the day for the birds' takeoff arrived, the entire flock of three hundred ducks gathered into one living mass on the river. This was Mother Duck's last time together with Grey Neck, and she counseled the young duck on what to do when the rest of them were gone.

"Keep close to that shore where a spring runs into the river," she said. "Sometimes the water doesn't freeze there the whole winter, and as long as you can swim in it you'll be safe." Then Mother Duck heard the loud command from the old leader.

"Ready, take off!" And she joined the flock as the ducks rose into the air.

For a long time, after Grey Neck was left alone on the river, she followed with her eyes the disappearing formation of the ducks.

11

The river on which Grey Neck paddled ran through mountains covered with dense forest. In the mornings the water began to freeze around the edges, and in the daytime the ice, thin as fine glass, would melt.

"Can it be that the whole river will freeze over? " Grey Neck wondered. "Where will I swim then? What will I do?"

The river was empty and silent now. Grey Neck looked towards the forest where she could hear the grouse making whistling sounds and rabbits and squirrels jumping here and there in the dim light.

One day she summoned up her courage and went into the forest. But as soon as she stepped in, she suffered a terrible fright. Right in front of her, Rabbit rolled out in a heap from under the bushes. He was shaking like a poplar leaf as he mumbled:

"How you frightened me! My heart dropped to my stomach." At the sight of Grey Neck, he soon calmed down. "What are you doing here? The ducks have all flown away long ago!"

"I cannot fly. Fox bit my wing and broke it when I was still quite little."

"I know Fox. The worst scoundrel! He's been after me, too. You watch out for him, especially when the river gets covered with ice. He'll sneak up on you."

So Grey Neck and Rabbit made friends. Rabbit was just as unprotected as Grey Neck and was able to save his life only by staying always on the run.

"If only I had wings like a bird, then I wouldn't be afraid of any one in the world. And you, even without wings, are still able to swim and dive into the water whenever you want to. But I have no way to escape my enemies. In the summer I can at least hide, but in the winter every place is open."

When the first snow fell, the river still held out; the part that froze in the night was broken up by the moving water later. But that soon changed. The ice became stronger.

One quiet starry night the trees in the forest were standing silently on the banks of the river like a guard of giants. The mountain seemed taller. The moon, high above, splashed everything with sparkling light. And the river, so turbulent in the daytime, became subdued. Then, the frost crept up, hugged the river tightly and covered her with glistening glass.

Grey Neck was in despair. The only part of the river not frozen now was a pool in the middle. And what Grey Neck feared more than anything actually happened.

Fox appeared on the shore.

"Ah, an old acquaintance, I see. How do you do!" Fox spoke in an unhurried and unworried manner. "Haven't seen you for quite a while." Fox gave Grey Neck a quick look. "Oh-ho! You've grown. Well, I just stopped by to wish you a good winter."

"I don't wish to see you," Grey Neck answered and closed her eyes. "Go away. Please go away!"

"If that's the way you feel," Fox replied, ever so agreeably, "I'll say 'so long' for now."

When Fox went away, Rabbit ambled towards Grey Neck and said, "Watch out, Grey Neck. Fox will come again." Then Grey Neck began to feel as frightened as Rabbit.

She could not even enjoy the special winter beauty all around her. She hardly noticed that all the earth was covered with snow carpets; the bare trees draped with silvery down; and the fat fir trees dressed in ermine coats. Grey Neck found no pleasure in the scene. Instead she trembled with fear that her pool would soon freeze over, and she would then have no place to go.

Fox came back in a few days. Standing on the bank of the river he tried to appear pleasant.

"Little Ducky, I am lonesome for you. Come over here!" Grey Neck didn't answer and Fox continued. "Well — if you don't want to come to me, I am not proud. I'll come to you!"

And Fox began to crawl slowly over the ice towards the pool. He couldn't get all the way to the water because the ice was still thin, and Fox was cautious. Licking his lips, he said, still pleasantly:

"You are a silly duck! Why don't you get out on the ice? You might as well." Grey Neck thrashed around in the small pool and dove down. "No? All right then — goodbye. See you tomorrow."

Fox came every day to see if the pool had frozen. The new frost, meanwhile, did its work. All that was left of the pool of water was a little window. The ice around it was strong enough for Fox to sit close to the edge of the water. Grey Neck felt more desperate than ever as she dove into the water and Fox sat on the very edge and chuckled. It was a mean, greedy chuckle.

"Go ahead and dive, I'll eat you just the same, you know." Grey Neck heard him; heard the final threat: "Better come out by yourself."

Rabbit saw from the shore what Fox was up to, and he bristled with anger.

"Oh, what a scoundrel — that Fox! He will gobble up the gentle Grey Neck! I am afraid he will!" But there was nothing he could do.

Helpless to save Grey Neck from her fate, Rabbit jumped out of his lair to forage for some food and to play with his rabbit friends. The frost was quite fierce, but the rabbits kept themselves warm by beating one paw against the other.

"Hey, fellows, watch out!" one of the rabbits suddenly signaled. Danger was under their very noses. On the edge of the forest stood a bent old hunter, who had slid quietly on his skis, ever so quietly, and was making up his mind which of the rabbits to shoot.

"Well, now, that's going to be a nice warm coat for the old woman," the old man was thinking, as he chose the fattest of the rabbits. He had already aimed the gun, but the rabbits spied him and instantly dashed into the forest.

"Oh, you rascals," the old man cried, angry at the rabbits. "I'll show you... Don't you understand that my old woman needs a fur coat? She can't go around freezing, for goodness' sake. And I want to tell you something: you aren't going to fool Ivanich, no matter how fast you run, because I, Ivanich, am smarter than you."

So old Ivanich started looking for the rabbits by following their tracks; but the smart rabbits had scattered over the forest like dry peas — no tracks left to follow. The hunter soon tired and sat down on the bank of the river to rest.

"My dear old woman, our fur coat ran away," he was still thinking aloud. "I'll just rest here a bit, then go look for another."

The old hunter was sitting there, feeling sorry about losing the rabbits, when suddenly, before his eyes, Fox crawled over the frozen river, crouching like a cat.

"Good gracious, what's this! A fox!" The old man was thrilled. "That would make a fine collar for the old woman's fur coat. I'll start with the collar and worry about the coat later," he mumbled. "I wonder why the fox came here? He must have gotten thirsty. On the other hand, he might have taken a notion to catch a fish in the little pool."

Fox, meanwhile, had crawled right up to the water where Grey Neck was swimming and lay down on the ice.

The old man's eyes weren't so good any more and he didn't notice the duck behind the fox. "I must be careful how I shoot," the old man thought, as he aimed his gun at Fox, "for the old woman will scold if she finds holes in her collar." He aimed for a long time — choosing a right place. At last he fired.

Through the smoke, the old man saw how something darted over the ice. He ran over, falling twice before he reached the pool. What he found made him open his mouth. There wasn't a trace left of the fox collar; just as if it had never existed.

Instead, there was frightened little Grey Neck swimming in the tiny pool.

"What's this?" exclaimed the old man, spreading his hands out in bewilderment. "The first time I ever saw a fox turn into a duck. What a sly one!" The man shook his head and tried to figure out what had happened. "That fox I saw must have run away...Ah, me. No collar for your fur coat, old woman. What am I to do now?" the man moaned.

"But what about you, little duck? Why are you swimming here now?" He spoke kindly, taking a close look at little Grey Neck. "Oh, poor thing, you have a broken wing, I see."

Grey Neck did not feel afraid of old Ivanich, so she came out of the water and went towards him. "Oh, you foolish thing, you. You'll either freeze to death here or that fox will eat you! Of course!" He touched the duck gently and wondered what to do next.

The old man thought a while, shaking his head. "I know what I'll do, I'll take you home to my grandchildren. They'll be glad to have you for a pet. And in the spring, you'll lay eggs for the old woman, and hatch some ducklings, maybe. Right?"

The old man picked up the duck and put her inside his big coat. Saved from the frost and the fox, Grey Neck snuggled against the warm wool.

So the old woman did not get her rabbit fur coat. Fox did not get his duck dinner. The fur coat did not get its fox collar. But the grand-children did get a pet for themselves.

And little Grey Neck is safe.

Designed by Barbara Holdridge
Composed by Brown Composition, Inc., Baltimore,
Maryland in Souvenir and Baskerville
Printed on acid-free paper and bound in Singapore
through Palace Press